MW00748474

whoopee!

For little cowpokes everywhere and Buzz.

Published in 2004 by Simply Read Books Inc.
www.simplyreadbooks.com

Cataloguing in Publication Data

Czernecki, Stefan, 1946-
Ride'em cowboy / cwritten and illustrated by Stefan Czernecki. --
1st ed.

ISBN 1-894965-06-X

1. Cowboys--Juvenile fiction. I. Title

PS8555.Z49R44 2004 jC813'.54 C2004-900028-4

The cowboy carvings photographed to illustrate this book are from Stefan Czernecki's collection. They were made by Martin Schatz (1911-1994), a rancher and cowboy from Cowely, Alberta . The patchwork quilt, pillow, and chair cushion were made by Pauline Lawson, and the buildings were made by Jim Allan.

While every effort has been made to obtain permission to use material there may be cases where we have been unable to trace the creator. The publisher will be happy to correct any omission in future printings.

Thanks to the following people for their help in the preparation of this book: Tiffany Stone, Tim Rhodes, Paul Beckett, Laurence Tessier, Gail Carscallen, Marion Leithead, Michael Misuraca.

Printed in China

10 9 8 7 6 5 4 3 2 1

Book Design Elisa Gutiérrez
Photography Mia Cunningham
Scan Separations ScanLab

Stefan Czernecki

Ride 'Em, Cowboy

Simply Read Books

cock-a
Rooster's crowin'.
Sun's risin'.

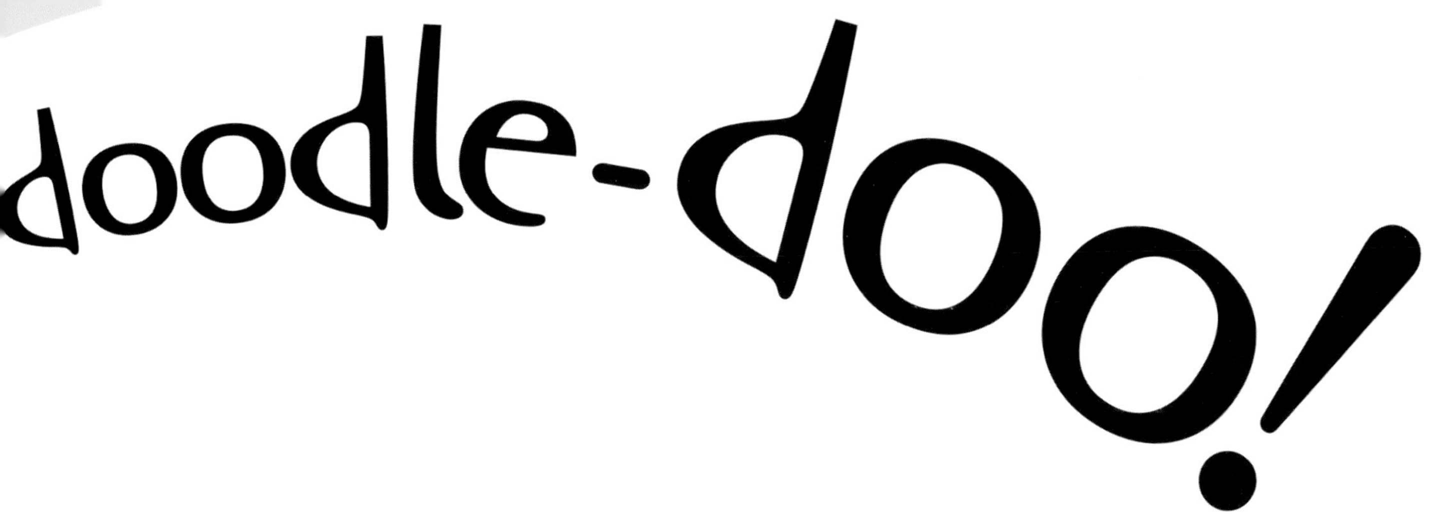

Time for the ranch day to begin.

Cowboys saddle up their horses.
Ride out on the range.

cloppety
clop!

Twirl their ropes in the air.

Yippee yiyo kiyay!

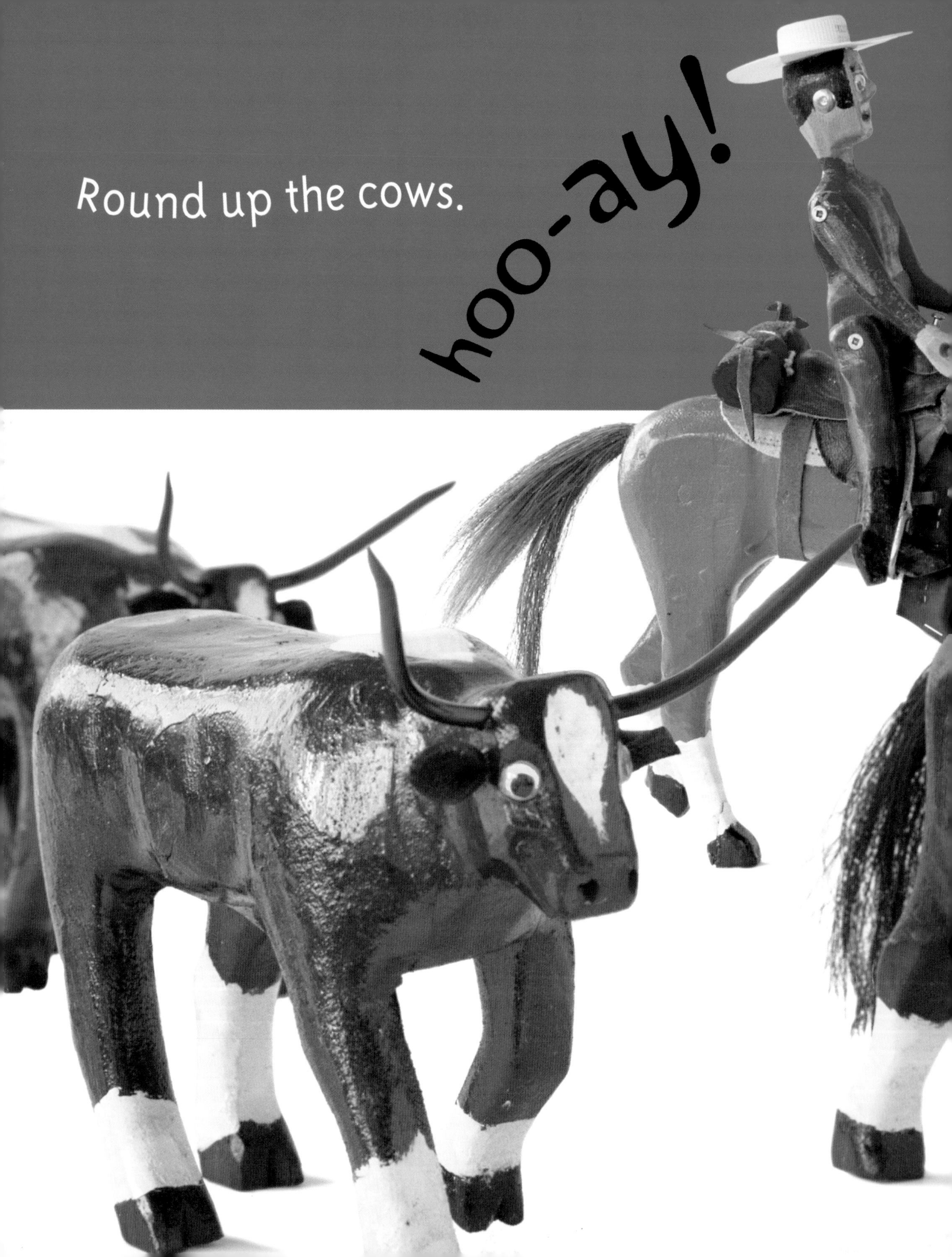
Round up the cows.
hoo-ay!

hoo-ay!

Rope little dogies.

Ok.

Brand the new calves.

It don't hurt 'em they say.

Tame wild horses.

Whoa, boy!
Whoa!

Ride buckin' broncos.
yeeee-

Yahoo!

Wrestle stampedin' steers.

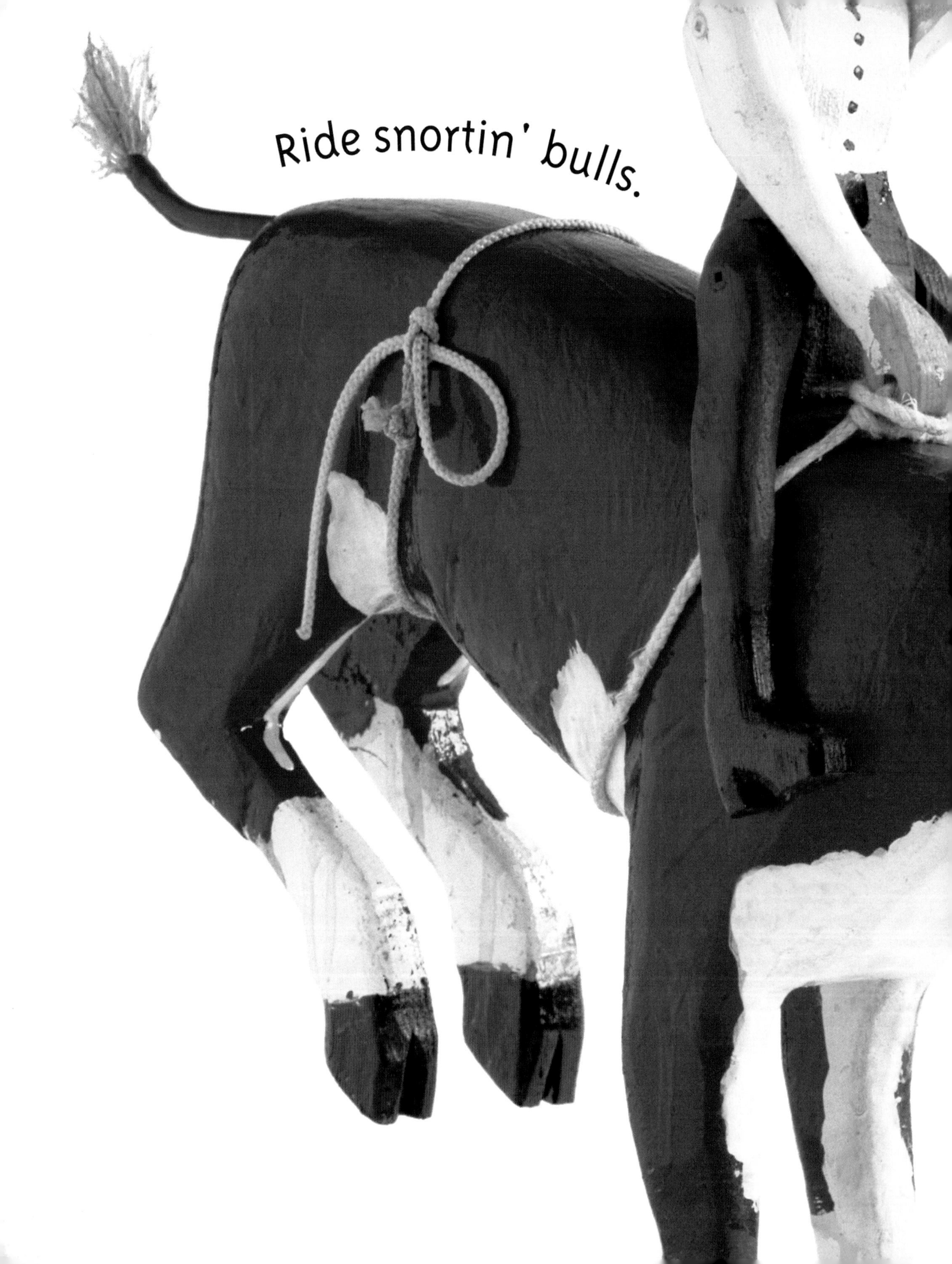

Ride snortin' bulls.

whoopee!

Ride jumpin' jack rabbits.

Why not?

Milk the cows.

no way!

Rope struttin' turkeys.

oray!

Herdin' and ropin'

and brandin' are done.

End of the cowboys' workin' day.

Ride into town.

Kick up their heels.

Square dancin' and singin'

and spendin' their pay.

hoo-hoo-hoo-hoo!

Owl's hootin'. Moon's risin'.

Gettin' late.

Cowboys head home
and hit the hay.
Dream of ridin' rodeo
someday.

Whoopee!

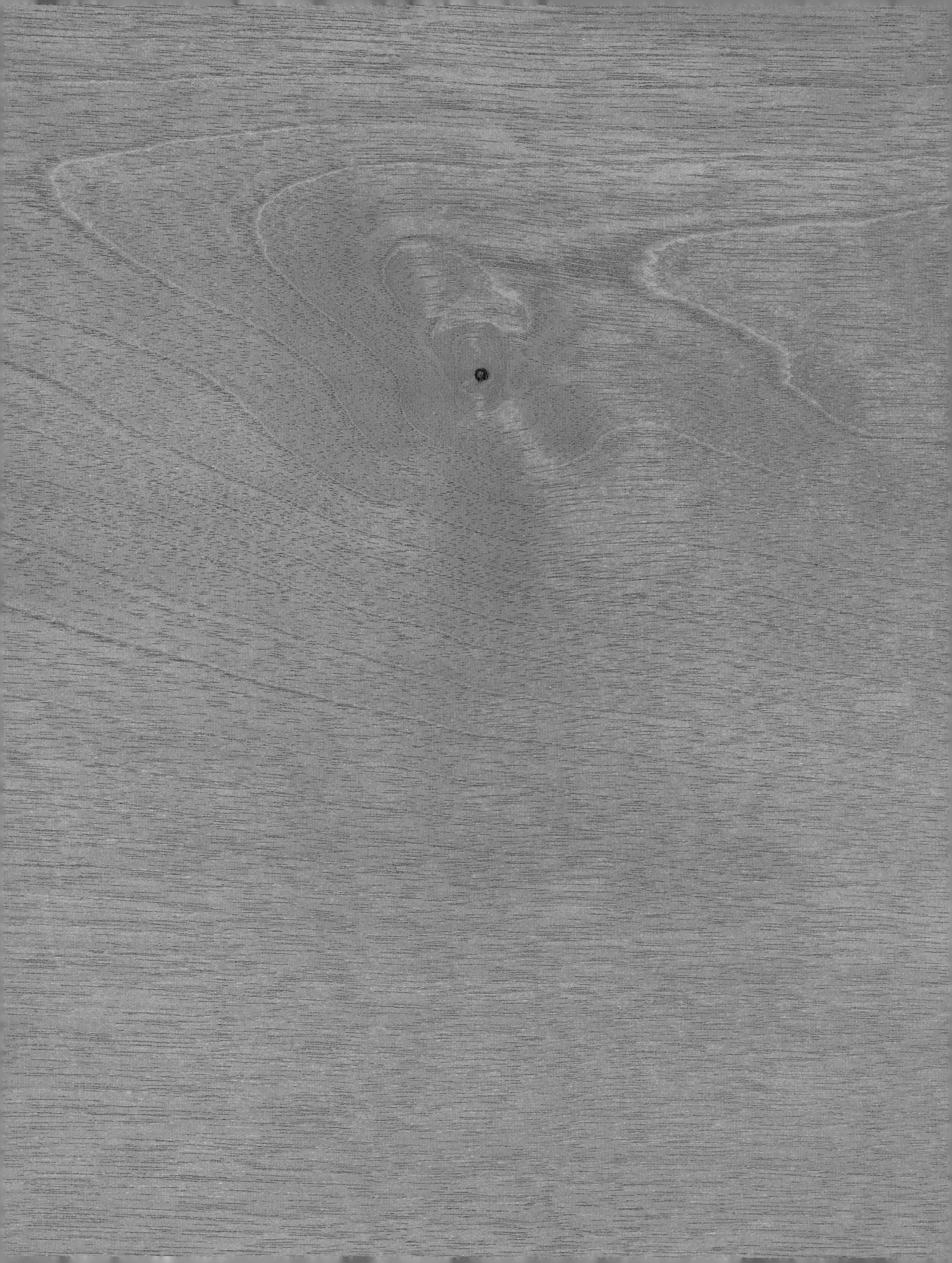